KT-555-941

WITHDRAWN FROM STOCK

ROCK RIVER STORIES 2

LITTLE OBIE
== and the ==
KIDNAP

*There was Mrs Jumping Joseph with the
two Cutlers having their dinner.*

ROCK RIVER STORIES 2

LITTLE OBIE AND THE KIDNAP

Written by
MARTIN WADDELL

Illustrated by
ELSIE LENNOX

WALKER BOOKS
LONDON

For Henry and Edward

C5040 778 99

AV
/JF/F

First published 1991 by
Walker Books Ltd, 87 Vauxhall Walk
London SE11 5HJ

Text © 1991 Martin Waddell
Illustrations © 1991 Elsie Lennox

The right of Martin Waddell to be identified as author
of this work has been asserted by him in accordance
with the Copyright, Designs and Patents Act 1988.

First printed 1991
Printed in Great Britain by
Richard Clay Ltd, Bungay, Suffolk

British Library Cataloguing in Publication Data
Waddell, Martin
Little Obie and the kidnap.
I. Title II. Lennox, Elsie
823'.914[J] PZ7

ISBN 0-7445-2208-0

CONTENTS

"They're useful, Little Obie
and that Marty," said Grandad.

LITTLE OBIE AND THE RESCUE

The winter after Marty Hansen came to live with Little Obie and his grandparents in their cabin at Cold Creek on the Rock River was one bad winter.

It blew blizzards and it snowed and it snowed and it snowed. Grandad got a chill and Little Obie's grandma, Effie, had to nurse him and rub him. They would have shivered if Marty and Little Obie hadn't got busy on Moose Ridge chopping.

"They're useful, Little Obie and that Marty," said Grandad.

"Sometimes is," said Effie. "Sometimes isn't," but inside herself she was pleased at the way they chopped and sawed and pulled and worked about the place, all winter long.

When spring came Grandad and Effie and Little Obie and Marty Hansen got busy on Moose Ridge, clearing it for growing. They had to lug the old tree stumps out of the ground, and they had to go rooting. It took a long time, but they managed it all by themselves, just like they did everything else, because there wasn't anyone else to help them.

That is the way it was at Cold Creek until the time Little Obie went down to Yellow Springs, and that changed everything.

It happened this way.

One day Grandad and Little Obie went down in the wagon to Bailey's Ford, which wasn't just the biggest place around, it was the only place. They were in Mr Hannigan's store for provisions and Mr Hannigan said,

"Reckon I could use that boy, Obadiah."

"I can use him myself," Grandad said.

"Reckon I *need* him," said Mr Hannigan.

"What do you need Little Obie for?" Grandad asked.

"Got to do some fetching, down at Yellow Springs," Mr Hannigan said. "There ain't nobody here man-sized that can be spared, so I thought: that Obie, he may be little, but he can handle himself like a grown man. The next time Obadiah comes in from Cold Creek, I'll ask after him."

Grandad thought a bit. He didn't know what Effie would think about lending Little Obie to Mr Hannigan, when they had the barn-building to be done, up on the Ridge.

"The only other one who can be spared is Mrs Jumping Joseph," said Mr Hannigan. "She's man enough, but you can't expect me to spend days and nights in the wagon with that wild old wood bear!"

"Well..." said Grandad, and that was that. Little Obie wanted to go, because he hadn't been out of the Rock River Valley before and he thought it would be a big adventure, one that would show Marty Hansen who was top dog. Effie hummed and hawed and didn't say yes and didn't say no, but in the end Little Obie was to go. In return Mr Hannigan gave Grandad all the bolts and nails and iron work that he needed for the barn, so it was a good deal for everybody, or it seemed so.

"I'd have been more use than Obie!" Marty Hansen said, when she heard.

"I need you at home, girl!" said Effie.

"I should have been born a boy!" Marty grumbled, but there wasn't any way she could talk herself into it when Effie didn't

*One time Mr Hannigan banged the table
with his big fist.*

Well, they went and got there, but that is not the story.

Taylor's Post at Yellow Springs wasn't like Little Obie thought it would be. It was stuck out in the middle of nowhere, just the Post and a few old cabins and corrals for the cattle men passing through, only there weren't any of them there then, so Little Obie didn't see them.

They were a longer time at Taylor's Post than they should have been, on account of Mr Taylor and Mr Hannigan not seeing eye to eye on what was a fair deal. One time Mr Hannigan banged the table with his big fist and set Little Obie to load all the stuff back on the wagon, saying they'd go somewhere else, but in the end Little Obie had to load it all off again when the two men agreed and shook on it, like they always knew they would. There wasn't really any place to go,

except Aaron Howitzer's or Yeovil Bend, and there was too much that needed doing at Bailey's Ford for Mr Hannigan to be going all that way on his wagon.

The trading was done, and the talking that came after it, and then they set off home on

the wagon. They were a day and a night away from Taylor's Post and crossing Goose Spit when they came upon the Cutlers, or what was left of them.

It wasn't pretty, what they saw. A mile or two another way and they wouldn't have seen it, and then the Cutlers would have died.

It was Little Obie who saw them first.

They were off the trail, and down below the ridge at Minter's Rock. At first Little Obie thought it was some wagon with the axle broken that got left behind, but then he knew that it wasn't, so he woke Mr Hannigan.

Mr Hannigan wasn't too pleased, but they had to go to help because they couldn't leave people like that, out in the middle of nowhere, maybe sick or hurt.

"We'll take a look, boy," Mr Hannigan said, and they did.

The Cutlers' ox died, and that was what had stopped their wagon. Mrs Cutler was sick already when that happened, and Mr Cutler was in a fix. He drew the wagon in by the shade of the rock near the river, and then he went off to get help, if he could find it. Nobody knows what happened to him, but Minter's Rock is a long way from nowhere and he was an old man. Maybe he just wasn't strong enough to make it.

The two little ones and Mrs Cutler had food and water, and Mr Cutler had fixed them a shelter to hide from the sun in, spreading the canvas out from the wagon, but they waited too long, and Mrs Cutler died.

When Little Obie and Mr Hannigan found them, Ham and Ezekiel Cutler were nearly dead themselves. They just lay there. Neither of them could talk, they were so weak.

Mr Hannigan and Little Obie didn't do much talking either. They got busy doing, because what needed to be done needed doing fast.

They hitched one of the horses to the Cutlers' wagon to take the place of their ox, and they drove the two wagons on as fast as

they could, with Mr Hannigan on one and Little Obie on the other, and the two small children made as safe as they could in the back. They got the Cutlers to Bailey's Ford all right, without Ham or Ezekiel dying, but then nobody knew what to do about the two children.

That's when Mrs Jumping Joseph took over.

Mrs Jumping Joseph was a little whiskery woman, no bigger than a child's size, but tough as an old boot. Some said she was a hellfire preacher's wife, and some said that Mr Jumping Joseph was a claim-jumper at the gold fields who got hanged for his trouble, but no one knew exactly where Mrs Jumping Joseph came from, or how she got to Bailey's Ford. One day she just turned up. She built a shack down by the Black Rocks at Hannigan's Creek that was half a house and half a cave. She did a bit of fishing and a bit of trapping and a bit of panning in the Creek and a bit of hard heaving if anybody needed a hand and didn't mind putting up with her ways.

Mrs Jumping Joseph walked in on everybody wondering what to do with Ham and Ezekiel Cutler, and she grabbed the two little ones as if she was their mother.

"Ain't never had no children," she told Mr Hannigan. "Looks like I got some now!"

"Them children can't be brought up in a cave!" Collie Gaines said, but she didn't say it to Mrs Jumping Joseph's face. There wasn't one of them at Bailey's Ford who would risk the edge of the old wood-woman's tongue.

"Don't see what's to be done!" said Mr Brover, shaking his head.

"I can't ask Effie to take on no more children," said Grandad. "We have an extra mouth to feed as it is, since young Marty Hansen's Pa died."

"You and Effie did all that could be asked of you, and more, Obadiah." Collie Gaines said. "But just the same, it don't seem right leaving those two children with that old woman in a bear cave."

The upshot of it all was that Mr Hannigan

"Ain't never had no children,"
Mrs Jumping Joseph told Mr Hannigan.

fixed up the broken-down shed at the back of the sawmill for Mrs Jumping Joseph, so she could keep the children there till they had their strength, and then maybe something better could be figured out. Nobody thought the old woman would stick to it.

But Mrs Jumping Joseph did.

She settled in and cared for the two Cutlers like a bear mother with her cubs. Everybody kept muttering that it wasn't right, but nobody offered anything better, and Mrs Jumping Joseph didn't act as if she was going to let the children go.

"I don't like it, Obadiah," Effie said.

Grandad didn't say nothing.

"Somebody needs to do some thinking!" Effie said.

"Reckon we just wait and see how things turn out," Grandad said.

"Hmmph!" said Effie.

Little Obie talked to Marty about it.

"Mrs Jumping Joseph, she killed a bear once, down Brady's mountain," he said. "She can chop wood like any man, and she can fist fight too, Mr Hannigan says, and that is why they're afraid of her. I don't see why she shouldn't take care of them Cutlers."

"Well, *you* don't see most things," said Marty. "There's nothing much unusual about that!" Little Obie chased her all the way to the Owl Pool, only when they got there Marty pushed him in, not the other way around!

That is just the way the two of them were, but they liked each other, and Little Obie could swim like a fish, so it didn't matter. They had Grandad and Effie to turn to when there was trouble, and that was what mattered. Effie and Grandad weren't wild, like Mrs Jumping Joseph.

*"She can't take them back in
the woods,"* Effie said.

LITTLE OBIE
AND THE
MUD FIGHT

Mrs Jumping Joseph didn't stick it long at the sawmill. One day she upped and left, taking the two little Cutler children with her.

"She can't take them back in the woods," Effie said.

"She just did!" Grandad said.

"Mrs Jumping Joseph never had no children of her own, and she can't hardly look after herself," said Effie, rocking back and forward in her chair.

"She's been looking after herself longer than you or me!" Grandad pointed out.

"Hmmmmmph!" said Effie, picking at her thread, for she was busy sewing, her old needle slipping in and out like lightning through the stiff cloth.

"Anyway, there ain't nothing anybody can do about it," Grandad said. "She's been and up and gone back to her old place at Black Rocks, so that's decided."

"Maybe so, and maybe not," said Effie.

There was a lot of talk about the place, but nothing happened.

Leastways, nothing happened, save for the digging, the hewing of wood, the caring for the hogs, the clearing of the ground, the putting up of the barn walls and the raising of the roof. Everybody round the place took a hand in what was going on and suddenly there was a month gone by. Then Mrs Wally Stinson drove over in the wagon for a long talk with Effie, and then she went away again.

It was Marty who brought back the next

news of the Cutlers and Mrs Jumping Joseph.

Marty was down helping Collie Gaines after Collie had three babies all at one time. Collie was snowed under with all that many babies and the four children she had already, which is a bit much for any woman with a harvest to get in. Marty was there helping, when she came upon Mrs Jumping Joseph down by the river, with the two Cutlers, and they were having their dinner.

"Chewing bones, and tearing at them with their teeth!" she told Effie in the wagon, on their way back from Gaines' place.

Effie wasn't one bit pleased.

"Mrs Jumping Joseph yelled at me," Marty said and she told Effie what Mrs Jumping Joseph yelled. Effie told Marty to go and wash her mouth out, it was that bad.

The next day Effie didn't work at Cold Creek. Instead she went off in the wagon down to Bailey's Ford, where she met up with Mrs Wally Stinson and Mrs Curley. They went to the river by Gaines' place where Marty had seen Mrs Jumping Joseph and the Cutler children, but by that time they had moved on. There was only the fire bed to mark where they had been, and the raw bones they had left behind them. So that was no use.

"Trailing round the woods, somewhere," Effie told Grandad.

"You won't find that old bear if she don't want you to." said Grandad. "Just bide your time and wait until she goes back to the Black Rocks, where she usually hangs out."

Effie still wasn't pleased, but there was nothing she or the other ladies could do about it but wait, and listen to the stories people kept telling about the old woman and the Cutler children.

One time Mrs Jumping Joseph was up at Van Helier's Rock and Ham fell off it. He could have been killed, but Mrs Jumping Joseph got him out somehow, with nothing broken.

Then Ham came into Hannigan's store and he did something and Mr Hannigan chased him and Ham shouted things at Mr Hannigan.

Little Ezekiel got his leg burned tending the fire when Mrs Jumping Joseph wasn't there, and another time Ezekiel fell in the

Creek and would have been drowned but
Mr Gaines got him out. Ezekiel was crying,
and Mrs Jumping Joseph turned up and
told Mr Gaines off for interfering and there
was trouble and trouble and trouble, with

the Cutlers following Mrs Jumping Joseph everywhere.

Mr Brover got mad at Ham and Ezekiel and said he'd set the dogs on them and Mrs Jumping Joseph came out to his place and fired her old rifle through his door and called him names. It was that bad.

One bother after another.

"Mrs Jumping Joseph ain't no lady!" Marty told Little Obie.

"How do you know she ain't no lady?" Little Obie asked.

"'Cause I know what she called Mr Brover, and no lady would call no gentleman a thing like that, and I'm not telling you what it was because you are too little," Marty said.

But it was Little Obie who went into Bailey's Ford with Effie, the time of the mud fight.

Effie and Mrs Brover and Mrs Wally Stinson were going to sort things out, because the trouble about the Cutler children couldn't be allowed to go on.

"We're having a talk with Mrs Jumping Joseph, Little Obie," Effie said. "Now you see you get hold of them two small Cutlers and keep them out of the way while we're doing our talking."

They went down to the Black Rocks, where Mrs Jumping Joseph's place was, but the business didn't turn out the way the ladies had planned it when they were talking it over in Mrs Brover's place.

"Mrs Jumping Joseph, she started yelling and hollering at Effie!" Little Obie told Marty later.

"What was she hollering?" Marty asked.

"Well, I'm not telling you, because you are a girl," Little Obie said, and then he told

33

Marty that the hollering wasn't the interesting part. The interesting part was when Mrs Wally Stinson said they couldn't stand by and watch two children being brought up like animals. Mrs Jumping Joseph went after Mrs Wally Stinson and pushed her in the river. Mrs Jumping Joseph was yelling and waving her fists and the two Cutlers got the river mud and they were pelting Effie and Mrs Brover and Mrs Wally Stinson.

Little Obie was pelting right back and he got Ham Cutler in the eye with a mudball and then Mrs Jumping Joseph went after him. She was roaring and shouting and firing her hunting rifle and the end of the story was that Effie and the two ladies and Little Obie all had to high tail it away from the Black Rocks, with the old bear woman dancing around behind them and shouting names, and Ham and Ezekiel Cutler shouting too, copying her.

"Seems like your deputation got a ducking, Ephemia!" Mr Hannigan said when they got back to the Ford, where he had been hanging around waiting for them.

"Seems like somebody gave somebody a chasing!" said Mr Brover, and they started laughing at Effie and the others.

"Seems to *me* that it is all left to the women!" said Effie. "You should all be ashamed of yourselves." Then she upped on the wagon with Little Obie, and drove back to Cold Creek.

That is what Little Obie told Marty.

"What is a deputation?" Marty asked, because she didn't know.

"When somebody doesn't like something somebody's doing and they gang up their friends and they go and tell the somebody so," said Little Obie. "Like Effie and the ladies trying to tell Mrs Jumping Joseph that she can't bring up them two small Cutlers like that."

Marty thought a while. "*Nobody* smacks your grandma with mud balls," she told Little Obie.

"Well, Mrs Jumping Joseph did," said Little Obie.

Marty told Grandad about it.

"Is that so?" Grandad said.

"That is what Little Obie *says* is so," said Marty. "Only I don't know if it is."

Grandad didn't say anything for a moment.

Then he said, "Sounds *serious* to me!" but the way he said it was half concerned, and half laughing.

That didn't stop Marty worrying.

Effie was out on the ridge chopping wood and you could tell by her chopping that she was cross. She was banging and banging at the wood, taking it out on *somebody* for making her look foolish in front of Mr Hannigan and the men.

"There will be more trouble yet about them Cutlers!" Marty told Little Obie.

And there was.

Nobody could mud-ball Effie and get away with it.

Effie wasn't made that way.

*Little Obie stayed put, and didn't say anything,
waiting for them to go away.*

LITTLE OBIE
AND THE
KIDNAP

Little Obie had a hiding place he kept all to himself, behind the apple barrel in the barn, and sometimes he just went there and ate an apple and had a think. One day he was doing it, when Grandad and Effie came in the barn. Little Obie stayed put, and didn't say anything, waiting for them to go away.

"You can't do it, Effie!" Grandad said.

"Who can't?" said Effie.

"Well, you can't. It ain't the way things are done."

"I'm doing it, Obadiah!" said Effie. "Either you help me or you don't. I have a duty to those children, and there ain't no other way out of it."

Grandad stood there, and scratched his nose.

"You're a clever critter!" Effie said. "I reckon you knew it would come to this all along." She said it kind of cross, but she didn't sound cross, really. It sounded playful, as if Effie and Grandad were two little kids.

"Well, maybe I did and maybe I didn't," said Grandad. "It didn't seem right asking you, with Marty here already."

"Hmmmph!" said Effie. "Maybe so."

Just then Grandad spotted Little Obie behind the barrel. Little Obie was hunkered right down, because he didn't think he should be listening, but he wanted to hear just the same. He didn't know he was spotted until Grandad got him by the breeches and dragged him out.

"Rattlesnake!" said Grandad, and he gave Little Obie a shake.

"That's a mean, nasty thing to be doing, Little Obie," said Effie. "Listening to what folks say."

"I wasn't!" said Little Obie. "Leastways I didn't mean to."

"Lying don't help," said Grandad. "Lying only makes it worse."

"Little pitchers has big ears," said Effie to Grandad.

"The least said in front of either of them, the better," said Grandad. "Leastways, till we have it all figured out."

"That's so," said Effie, and she went about what she was doing, which was getting the straw for a mattress, and she didn't say another word.

"What do we want another mattress for?" Marty asked Effie, when Effie was stuffing it.

But Effie wouldn't say what for. She just kept on stuffing.

"Your grandma is acting like she's thinking something," said Marty.

So Marty tried Grandad.

Grandad was fixing and polishing his hunting gun that he kept on the wall by the door, where it was handy when he needed it.

"What do we want another mattress for, Grandad?" Marty asked.

"Better ask Effie, girl!" said Grandad, which wasn't much help.

The next time Little Obie and Marty were on their own out at the woodpile, they had a talk about it. Little Obie told Marty what-he-had-heard-behind-the-apple-barrel and Marty told Little Obie about the-mattress-we-don't-need-because-we-have-enough-of-them-already, and neither of them could puzzle it out.

"Your grandma is acting like she's *thinking* something," said Marty. "I never knew nobody with a mind for such *thinking* all the time."

"Well, Grandad does the *doing*," said Little Obie. "That's 'cause he is a man."

"Your grandma *does* too, when she's quit thinking," Marty said. "But she don't make so much fuss about what she is doing. Men are all fuss, and boys are worse!"

"I don't fuss much!" Little Obie objected.

"Don't do much neither," said Marty, and she went off with the wood she had cut which was twice as much as Little Obie had cut, because she had been *doing* while she was talking, and Little Obie had just been talking.

That was in the morning.

Late afternoon, they all got in the wagon and went to Bailey's Ford. Grandad and Effie had a talk with Mr Hannigan in his room at the back of the store, and Collie Gaines and old Gerd Weber and Mr Brover were all in it, talking and arguing, but Obie and Marty were sent outside, where they couldn't hear what was being said.

Then Mr Hannigan put on his hat, and he went off down by the Creek.

"Where's Mr Hannigan off to?" Marty asked Grandad.

"Bear hunting," said Grandad.

"He don't look like he was going bear hunting to me," said Little Obie.

"Bear trapping, more like it!" said Grandad. "Only it ain't no ordinary bear he's after, and it ain't no ordinary trap. Maybe he's going to get some old bear just where he wants her to be."

He wouldn't say anything else.

It was beginning to get dark when they got in the wagon, with the moon coming up behind the trees. Grandad and Effie were in front, with Marty and Little Obie behind.

They drove the wagon out towards the Gaines' place, but they didn't go there. Instead, Grandad slowed the horses, and pulled off the track near the turn in the river by the Black Rocks, and there they waited.

Grandad went off for a while, over the rocks, where he could look down to Bailey's Ford. He sat up there in the growing darkness where no one could see him, but he could see what he wanted to see.

He was waiting for a signal.

He must have got it, because when he came back to the wagon he said, "Time we were moving!" to Effie.

Effie climbed down off the wagon.

"You stay here and don't make a sound!" Grandad said to Little Obie and Marty.

Grandad and Effie went clambering off down the bank towards the river, where Mrs Jumping Joseph's old cave was.

They drove the wagon out towards the Gaines' place,
but they didn't go there.

It got darker, and then it got darker still. There was just the crash of the water rushing and the tree sounds, and nothing else. It was a little too creepy for comfort.

"Reckon I know what they're doing!" whispered Marty.

"Anybody knows that!" Little Obie whispered back.

"OK! *anybody* can tell me then!" said Marty. "You don't know, 'cause you are just little, and ain't smart like me."

"Well, I do know, so there!" said Little Obie, forgetting to whisper. "Grandad and Effie have gone to Mrs Jumping Joseph's to see her, and they are another deputation."

"Uh-uh!" said Marty, very grandly.

"What do you mean, 'uh-uh'?" said Little Obie, getting annoyed.

"Mrs Jumping Joseph ain't *there*," said Marty. "She's gone off with Mr Hannigan

back to the Ford. You can't have a deputation to somebody who ain't there."

"Well, you don't know what they're doing
then!" said Little Obie. "You know what
they're *not* doing. I don't call it smart,
pretending you know what you don't
know."

"You was the one pretending!" said
Marty.

"You know what I think?" said Little
Obie. "I think neither of us knows."

Then...

"Shush!" said Marty. "Somebody's coming."

There was a snapping and a cracking of
branches and undergrowth. Somebody was
coming through the darkness, in a hurry,
breathing heavily.

"Grandma?" Little Obie called softly.

But it wasn't Grandma.

It was Grandad, with a little struggling

bundle in his arms, which accounted for all the crashing and crackling. The bundle was Ham Cutler. Ham was kicking and fighting and making as much noise as he could, but he couldn't make much, because Grandad had his mouth muffled, and was holding him tight.

"All I could do to catch the varmint," Grandad muttered, and he dumped Ham in the wagon, telling Little Obie and Marty to take hold of the boy, so he couldn't leap out.

Marty got his head, and Little Obie sat on his middle, and they got Ham Cutler quieted, though he didn't like it.

Then Effie came. She had Ezekiel Cutler in her arms, curled up in a blanket fast asleep with his thumb in his mouth.

"You got the easy one!" Grandad grumbled.

Ezekiel was so small that he didn't wake

Marty got his head, and Little Obie
sat on his middle.

up, even though Ham was still crying and fussing a lot.

"What about Mrs Jumping Joseph?" Marty asked.

"Mrs Jumping Joseph ain't coming," said Grandad. "Leastways, I hope she ain't!"

And he hurried to start off in the wagon.

When they'd gone a ways Effie gave Ezekiel to Marty to hold, and she got in the back of the wagon and started talking to Ham. She was talking to him and persuading him but all the time holding on to him, so he couldn't squirm out of the back of the wagon and go running off.

They got all the way back up the trail to Cold Creek in the darkness and by the time they'd got there Ham had given up crying, but he wasn't talking much. He didn't open his mouth when they got him in the cabin. Effie had the new stuffed mattress in the loft, and they put Ham and Ezekiel up there. Effie stayed with them till they were safe and sound and well asleep, and Grandad stayed down below with Marty and Little Obie talking.

"It was a bad thing to do, but it had to be done," Grandad said. "I don't like it. Nobody does, least of all little Ham. But Ham and Ezekiel were running wild, with only that old woman to look after them."

Marty looked worried.

"Well, now we're looking after them," said Grandad. "You and me and Effie."

"How?" said Little Obie.

"You'll do a bit, Marty'll do a bit, I'll do a bit and Effie'll do a lot, the way she always does," said Grandad. "Leastways, they can't be worse off than they were before."

"Ham don't think so," said Marty. "I don't reckon he'll stay."

"He's too small and scared not to," said Grandad. "It's a long, long way back, and he don't know the way, and he wouldn't go without Ezekiel, so he won't. We'll keep an eye on him just the same, but I reckon Ham'll settle."

"We're kidnappers!" Little Obie said.

Then Marty said, "What about Mrs Jumping Joseph?"

Grandad didn't say anything for a minute. He just sat there looking at the fire, and when he did speak, he sounded sad.

"Well, I don't know what about Mrs Jumping Joseph, I reckon she won't miss them, now they're gone, and anyway she don't know where they've got to."

Grandad didn't sound too certain.

Neither did Effie, when she came down.

"Mrs Jumping Joseph," Little Obie said. "She's ... she's kind of mad, isn't she? What with living in the woods all alone?"

"Maybe so," said Effie.

"But she ain't a *bad* woman?" said Little Obie.

"No," said Effie "Just…"

"Just like an old bear," said Marty.

"She ain't like other folks, Marty," said Grandad. "She's not able to look after them little Cutlers, even though she loves them. So we have got to do it for her."

Little Obie didn't say anything.

Neither did Marty.

And they went to bed, not feeling too good inside about what they had done.

Ham and Ezekiel Cutler cleaned up well,
once Effie got at them.

LITTLE OBIE AND THE GUN

Ham and Ezekiel Cutler cleaned up well, once Effie got at them.

She ducked them in the Creek and had the dirt off them, and she put them in proper clothes that had belonged to Little Obie once, when he was littler, only that was a long time ago, so the clothes felt clean and fresh. That was good, but it didn't make them happy.

Three times they went running away, but three times Grandad got them back. Ezekiel couldn't run far, on account of being so small, and Ham wouldn't leave him, and anyway they didn't know where they were properly, so Ham never had much of a chance.

It didn't stop them asking things about Mrs Jumping Joseph and where she was and when she'd be coming for them, and they didn't take kindly to getting no answer, or no proper answer that they could understand. They were just too small to make sense of what had happened, even Ham.

Effie started teaching them not to go round spitting, but she had to stop that, because Mrs Jumping Joseph had taught them how and it was their game to see who could spit the best. Effie reckoned there were other things that needed doing first, if they were going to settle down at Cold Creek and be happy. They could spit further than Little Obie, although he was much bigger than they were.

Ham and Ezekiel didn't seem to know what a bed was, or what a blanket was for, and they ran around wild any time they got the chance. Marty and Little Obie were worn out chasing after them and stopping them from running off to find Mrs Jumping Joseph or maybe drowning themselves in the Owl Pool. They were scary to take care of because they didn't seem to be afraid of anything.

"That old woman!" Effie told Grandad. "She has turned those two into wild creatures, just like herself."

Grandad was worried about Mrs Jumping Joseph, so he went into Bailey's Ford to see what had happened when she found the children gone, and whether she was forgetting them the way he'd said she might, although he didn't really believe it. Mrs Jumping Joseph wasn't there. She'd gone back to Hannigan's and made a row when she found out how she'd been tricked over the kidnapping, and she had bad-mouthed

*Mrs Jumping Joseph went off into the woods
the way she used to.*

Mrs Brover and Collie Gaines. She went around for a day or two hunting for her children and shouting and yelling and hollering at anyone there was to shout and yell and holler at, and then she just disappeared. She went off into the woods the way she used to, and nobody knew where she'd gone, or whether she would ever come back. She didn't own anything but her gun and the clothes she stood up in, so there was nothing to take with her or leave behind her.

That is what Grandad told Effie and Marty and Little Obie when he got back from the Ford, and nobody liked it. They were sorry for Mrs Jumping Joseph, but at the same time they were a bit frightened of her, and scared of what would happen if she found out where her children had gone.

"It *needed* doing, Obadiah," Effie kept

*Effie went and made a special
chicken and berry pie.*

insisting. "What has to be done, has to be done."

"Only the two Little Cutlers don't understand that," said Grandad. "They ain't happy. Maybe we shouldn't have done it."

"They'll forget soon enough," said Effie.

And she went and made a special chicken and berry pie, but it didn't do any good.

Ham and Ezekiel still went on asking after Mrs Jumping Joseph, but Mrs Jumping Joseph didn't show up.

At least, she didn't show up until she *did*, and then it was when no one was expecting her, because the word was that she was off somewhere in the woods below Bailey's Ford, but it turned out that she wasn't. She had widened the circle of her hunt, when everybody was beginning to think that hiding the children far away up at Cold Creek had her fooled, because Cold Creek wasn't a place she would normally be.

Late one evening Ham and Ezekiel were in bed and Grandad and Effie and Marty were in the barn working when...

BANG!

Then...

BANG! BANG! BANG!

"Obadiah!" Effie said.

"You stay here," Grandad said, heading for the barn doors.

"Where's Obie?" Effie said.

"You don't move," Grandad said, and he went out of the barn.

Mrs Jumping Joseph was there with her rifle.

She pointed it at Grandad's middle.

"Don't shoot, Mrs Joseph," Grandad said.

"Sit down!" Mrs Jumping Joseph said.

Grandad sat down on the ground.

Mrs Jumping Joseph was there with her rifle.

"Not there!" Mrs Jumping Joseph said. "Roll round a little."

Grandad rolled round a little.

Then Mrs Jumping Joseph walked to the door of the barn and looked inside.

"Two more hideaways," she said. "Out!" And she wagged her rifle at Effie and Marty.

They came out of the barn.

"You sit down beside him," she said, waving her rifle round, and looking as though she might fire it off at any moment.

That is what Little Obie thought, anyway. He'd been down by the Owl Pool when he'd heard the bangs and he'd come running back, but he wasn't fool enough to run where the banging was. Instead, he'd taken to the trees, and come out at the side of the cabin.

He looked and he saw, and he knew he had to do something or they'd all be killed. So he headed for the side window, to get into the house, where Grandad's hunting rifle was.

"I come for my children," Mrs Jumping Joseph said. The funny thing was that she didn't yell or shout like she usually did. She said it quietly. Her old brown berry face was dead set, but her eyes were gleaming wild, and kind of teary. "I had a think about it and I nosed around till I figured where they was, and now I've come to collect them."

"They are not your children," Effie said, bravely.

Mrs Jumping Joseph swung the rifle round, so the barrel pointed straight at Effie.

"You say that again!" she said.

Effie went pale.

"They ain't your children, Mrs Joseph!" Effie said.

BANG!

Mrs Jumping Joseph didn't shoot Effie, but she almost did. She shot at the ground just beside Effie's foot, and the dirt went all over Effie's dress, but the bullet didn't harm her.

That's when Little Obie eased open the door of the cabin, and came out into the open with Grandad's hunting gun in his hands.

Little Obie didn't know how to shoot, but he had seen Grandad do it and he figured he could manage if he had to. He raised the gun, but then he saw Grandad looking straight at him, past Mrs Jumping Joseph, and Grandad moved his head a little as if he was saying "*no*".

So Little Obie didn't shoot. He stood there, waiting to shoot if he had to.

"They ain't your children, Mrs Joseph," Effie repeated.

"I took 'em, when nobody else would," Mrs Jumping Joseph said. "That makes them mine."

"Now listen here…" Grandad said.

"I ain't come here to talk with you, Obadiah!" Mrs Jumping Joseph said. "My business is with *her*. She's the one lied and schemed with Hannigan and tricked me out of the way and came with her wagon and stole my children."

"You don't know how to look after those children," Effie said.

Mrs Jumping Joseph swung the rifle close to Effie, and Effie stopped talking.

"I want my children," Mrs Jumping Joseph said. "Where are they?"

Effie shook her head.

Little Obie didn't know what to do. He was stuck there with Grandad's gun thinking he ought to fire it, but seeing

Grandad's eyes on him, telling him not to do it, but he couldn't figure why.

Grandad was thinking that if Little Obie fired the gun he would as likely hit Effie or Marty Hansen as he would the old woman because it was too heavy for a boy to fire straight, but Little Obie didn't know that.

He stood there hoping there would be some other way out of it all.

Then Effie did a brave thing.

Very slowly she got to her feet, and dusted herself down.

"You sit down," Mrs Jumping Joseph said, waggling her rifle.

"I may as well be shot standing up, as sitting down," Effie said.

Grandad got to his feet.

"Me too," he said.

Mrs Jumping Joseph started swearing, and calling them names.

*Obie stood there hoping there would be some
other way out of it all.*

"Don't you use them words in front of young Marty," Effie said.

Marty was still sitting down, not knowing what Effie and Grandad wanted her to do.

"You took my children!" Mrs Jumping Joseph said.

"And washed them and scrubbed them and fed them and clothed them, the way they ought to be washed and scrubbed and fed and clothed," Effie said.

"I did all right," Mrs Jumping Joseph said.

Her old chins had started to wobble, whiskers and all, and her jaw was working, and the two teeth she had left at the front were chattering.

"You'd better give me that rifle, Mrs Joseph!" Grandad said, and he stepped forward. Grandad reckoned when she hadn't shot them the first time, it meant she was never going to, but he didn't know if he was right, he just had to count on it. For a moment Mrs Jumping Joseph's back stiffened, and she looked as if she was going to fire her rifle off, but then she didn't.

"That's right," Grandad said, and he took the rifle from her.

Little Obie lowered Grandad's rifle. All of a sudden he found he was full of shivers, because he had been very frightened, but not able to be frightened, because he might have had to do something.

Mrs Jumping Joseph started to shake and quiver, and then she was crying like a baby and the next thing was that Effie came over to her and put her arms around Mrs Jumping Joseph. Effie hugged that little sobbing whiskery woman as tight as ever she hugged a child that was hurt.

"Mind now, Effie," Grandad said, opening Mrs Joseph's rifle and slipping the shells out.

*Effie hugged that little sobbing whiskery woman as
tight as ever she hugged a child that was hurt.*

"This is between her and me, Obadiah!" Effie said. And she took Mrs Jumping Joseph stumbling towards the cabin. They went by Little Obie, but neither of them paid any heed to him. He felt silly, standing there with Grandad's too-big-for-him gun in his hands.

"Little Obie?" Grandad said.

"I was scared, Grandad," Little Obie said.

"Me too," said Marty.

"Well, that makes all four of us, and Mrs Jumping Joseph too!" said Grandad. He took the gun away from Little Obie and unloaded it.

"What happens now, Grandad?" asked Marty.

"What do we do?" asked Little Obie.

"We don't do nothing," Grandad said. "We just go about our business."

"I'm still afraid of Mrs Jumping Joseph," Little Obie said.

"There ain't no call to be afraid of her any more, Little Obie," Grandad said. "There ain't no bad in her. She's old and she's a bit mad, but she looked after them Cutler kids the best way she could. I guess she loves them as much as me and Effie love you and Marty, only she don't know how to bring them up right."

"Maybe we could show her?" suggested Marty.

But they couldn't.

Mrs Jumping Joseph wasn't the kind to be house-trained.

So this is what happened.

Ham and Ezekiel Cutler stayed on, sharing the cabin with Grandad and Effie and Marty Hansen and Little Obie, and they were part of the family. But they had Mrs Jumping Joseph to love them as well. She didn't live in the cabin, but she got busy and built herself a hidey-hole out of trees and cow hides and dried mud, by the Cold Creek. She went her own way and lived her own life, now and then disappearing off into the woods the way she used to, but always coming back to her children. She didn't soften her tongue, or her ways, but she did the best she could after her fashion not to cross anybody.

"Well, she is a queer one," Grandad said. "But the way she loves them Cutler kids and the way they hanker after her it don't matter much. It is the loving that counts."

"So long as there is some fool to do the dirty work!" said Effie drily.

"I guess that's a kind of loving Mrs Jumping Joseph don't rightly understand," Grandad said.

"Maybe so," said Effie.

"She's teaching us to pan for gold!" Little

"I want to be real rich when I grow up,
and I'm going to be."

Obie said. "Me and Ham. Reckon we will find some gold in Cold Creek and then we will all be rich."

"We're rich already," said Grandad.

"Well, I don't reckon so!" said Little Obie, sounding surprised. "I want to be *real* rich when I grow up, and I'm going to be."

Marty looked at him.

"You don't understand *nothing*, Little Obie," she said.

That is how Mrs Jumping Joseph and Ham and Ezekiel Cutler came to join the family at Cold Creek, on the Rock River. There was no one else there but the seven of them, and maybe that is all that was needed.

THE

END